OLD THUNDER

AND MISS RANEY

by Sharon Darrow ✳ illustrated by Kathryn Brown

DORLING KINDERSLEY PUBLISHING, INC.

A Melanie Kroupa Book

DK
Ink

Dorling Kindersley Publishing, Inc., 95 Madison Avenue, New York, New York 10016
Visit us on the World Wide Web at http://www.dk.com

Dorling Kindersley books are available at special discounts for bulk purchases for sales promotions or premiums. Special editions, including personalized covers, excerpts of existing guides, and corporate imprints can be created in large quantities for specific needs. For more information, contact Special Markets Dept., Dorling Kindersley Publishing, Inc., 95 Madison Ave., New York, NY 10016; fax: (800) 600-9098.

Library of Congress Cataloging-in-Publication Data
Darrow, Sharon.
Old Thunder and Miss Raney / by Sharon Darrow; illustrated by Kathryn Brown.—1st ed.
p.   cm.   "A DK Ink book."
Summary: Miss Raney is determined to win a ribbon for her biscuits at the county fair until a tornado changes her plans.
ISBN 0-7894-2619-6   [1. Contests—Fiction.   2. Fairs—Fiction.]   I. Title.
II. Brown, Kathryn, ill.   III. Title.   PZ7.D2525 Ol 2000   99-462361   [E]—dc21

The illustrations for this book were painted with watercolor and pen and ink.
The text of this book is set in 16 point Fournier. Printed and bound in U.S.A.
First Edition, 2000
10 9 8 7 6 5 4 3 2 1

To Stephen, Kristen, Elizabeth,
and Stephanie Harmon
—S.D.
For Kate Koye and Sarah Kay,
and for good old Freckles
—K.B.

The morning of the Washita County Fair, I scrambled out of bed and threw a batch of what I hoped would be prize-winning Sooner Biscuits in the oven. "Raney," I told myself, "all that practice is about to pay off."

I tied on my sunbonnet and scooted out to wake up my horse.

"Thunder," I said, "this time we got it in the bag and sewed shut."

Old Thunder nodded as he gulped down a big breakfast of Dr. Horace's Old-Fashioned Feed.

Slim & Sue

Bea Clover

Me and Old Thunder had always wanted a Washita County Fair blue ribbon. Slim Bacon won for his hefty hogs. And Beatrice Clover for her giant sunflowers and her Dizzy Bea's Wild Honey. And Winnie Oates for her biscuits, tomatoes, melons, eggplant, and collard greens. What's more, her horse, Lightning, won the Washita County Fair plowhorse race every single year.

Winnie & Lightning

But for me and Old Thunder, there'd been no blue ribbons, not a one. Not for canning sour pickles, or baking apricot pies. Not for fiddling, or square dancing, or mixing up the best mess of chicken feed. Not for buggy racing or pulling plows. Not a win, place, or show for me or Old Thunder.

Raney & Thunder

But today would change all that. Today at the Washita County Fair, Old Thunder and I'd show up with the finest stack of biscuits those judges would ever hope to taste.

Why, fiddle-dee-dee! My recipe baking up right this minute was sure to yield the fluffiest, crustiest, sweetest-smelling biscuits ever.

I pumped myself a tall drink of water, then tried to catch the warm aroma drifting out from my kitchen window. I sniffed. It was warm, all right. Too warm.

"Horsefeathers!" Burning biscuits!

Well, I'd just have to stir up another batch, park myself in front of the oven, and take them out when they were just right.

I opened my flour bin. . . . "Empty?
Well, fiddle-dee-dee."

Then I pinned on my town hat and
scurried down to the barn to find Old
Thunder. Puffy black clouds rose along
the horizon. Looked like we were in
for it now—a hailstorm, for sure.

"Oh, pshaw!" I said, and stopped short. But Old Thunder
nudged my arm with his head. I knew he had a real big
hankering for us to get that blue ribbon, so I hitched up
my little buggy.

"Giddyup, Thunder."

Down the road a piece, we met Slim Bacon chasing his hog, Sue, out of Winnie's vegetable patch. "Sue-ee, weather's coming. Get on home!"

He took off his hat and nodded. "Looks like a storm, don't you say so, Miss Raney?"

"I do indeedy, Slim, but I plan to get to town and back ahead of it, bake my Sooner Biscuits, and see you at the fair."

Slim laughed and slapped his knee. "Well, you sure as shooting ain't a-going to make it."

"Horsefeathers," I said. "We'll see about that."

A little farther on, we met Winnie Oates saddling Lightning for the fair, her prize-winning vegetables bursting out of her wagon.

She hollered, "Raney, you better turn that horse right around. You're heading into a cloud."

"No, indeedy, Winnie." I sniffed the air, smelling rain. "I plan to get to town and back ahead of it, pop my prize-winning Sooner Biscuits into the oven, and see you at the fair."

Winnie laughed. "You'll never make it with a horse poky as Old Thunder."

"Fiddle-dee-dee," I said, tying my hat ribbons tighter as raindrops splatted the buggy. "Thunder, don't you pay her no nevermind."

And Old Thunder didn't. His hooves went *clop-clop-thunk-thunk, clop-clop-thunk-thunk,* steady as you please, while those dark clouds rumbled in over our heads.

As I hurried to Beatrice Clover's general store, splinters of rain pelted my face, icy and sharp.

"Giving up on the fair this year, dear Raney?" she asked as she climbed into her brand-new motorcar heaped high with flowers and jars of honey.

"My stars, no!" I said. "I just have to bake my blue-ribbon prize-winning Sooner Biscuits, then I'll hurry on over to the fair."

Beatrice Clover looked at Old Thunder. "With that slow horse?" She shook her head. "Raney, my dear, not everyone can be a winner."

I bought my sack of flour, shoved it into my old carpet bag, and snapped the latch—just as a bolt of lightning flashed across the sky.

With my heart beating like the bass drum in the Fourth of July parade, I jumped in the buggy and yelled, "Giddyup, Thunder."

Old Thunder put back his ears, skittered around, leaned forward—and settled into his walk. *Clop-clop-thunk-thunk.*

BOOM! I slapped my hands over my ears. Great sakes alive, right over our heads! "Hurry, Thunder," I yelled. Another streak of lightning. Rumbledy, rumbledy, *CRASH!*

Old Thunder neighed. He took one quick step, then another, and plodded on. *Clop-clop-thunk-thunk.*

The storm rushed in behind us, howling like a freight train into the station. One side of the buggy jerked. The other side dipped. I hunkered down and held on tight. Old Thunder froze in his tracks.

"Don't stop now," I screeched. "It's a *tornado*!" Whirling and howling, the wind swirled round and round and sucked us right up off the ground.

Faster than you could shake a stick at it, that old tornado had us spinning like a top.

We zigged and zagged through lightning and thunder; twirled and whirled through hail and rain.

"Horsefeathers, we're flying wrong side up!" I grabbed the buggy and hung on tight, but my bag fell out and went flying.

"Thunder, the flour! We got to save that flour!"

Pretty soon, I was meeting myself a-coming and a-going. Every time the flour bag zipped by, I stretched out an arm or crooked out a foot. Why, I even tried to catch it with my teeth.

Just when I thought I might reach it, Sue spun by, gobbling up Winnie's vegetables in a swirl of sunflowers and honey jars.

Then the wind slacked off.

"Oh, fiddle-dee-dee," I cried. "Get ready to crash."

But lo and behold, that old whirlwind flipped us over and we landed—
right side up.

As the twister skipped away across the cotton field and the wind died
down, I whispered, "Flour's gone—looks like we can just forget about
our blue ribbon."

Then I saw it. My carpet bag of flour falling with the rain,
heading for the deepest puddle in the barnyard. "Catch it, Thunder!"
Old Thunder cloppity-clopped the buggy over to the puddle—
and that flour fell in, neat as a pin.

Up at the house, I opened
the bag and . . . oh, my! A cloud of
flour puffed out and filled up my kitchen,
light and fluffy, storm sifted and ready to go.
Why, I had to run the mixing bowl through
the air just to catch it all.

I made a double batch, one for the fair and
one for Old Thunder and me.

Why, I do declare, those biscuits were so light, they floated right out of the oven and into my mouth. They tasted a bit unusual—airy and fresh as the fields in spring—

but Old Thunder loved them. Instead of his lunch of Dr. Horace's Old-Fashioned Feed, I gave him six biscuits and told him, "I don't care what anybody says, you'll always be a prize winner to me."

Washita County Fair

That afternoon at the fair, the sky cleared up fine, turning as bright and blue as a first-prize ribbon. Folks said the twister must have lit a fire under all us from around these parts.

Slim Bacon's prize hog got so fat eating Winnie's tornado-tossed garden vegetables, she took first *and* second prize. And Beatrice Clover won a ribbon for most unusual flower arrangement.

Slim and Sue

Bea Clover

But my biscuits. My biscuits. Even though my Sooner Biscuits were lighter than spring air and fluffier than white summer clouds, the judges just tasted and shook their heads. First prize went to Winnie, who had gone back home and whipped up a batch of her famous Lightning-Rise Biscuits. Still no blue ribbon for me.

I guess that goes to show, like Beatrice Clover always says, "Not everybody can be a winner."

I stroked Old Thunder's forehead, and he nuzzled my hand. At least *he* liked my biscuits.

"Here, Thunder." I fed him six more. His ears perked up. And we set out for home.

But as we passed the plowhorse race, Old Thunder skittered a few steps and sidled himself over to Lightning, who was prancing and dancing around like he'd already won that race.

BOOM! The starting gun.

Old Thunder jumped. His head jerked. Why, I nearly slid out of the saddle when Old Thunder reared up and stampeded off behind the other horses.

Cloppity-cloppity. "Good old boy!"

We ripped by the grandstand—*cloppity-clippity*. The crowd yelled and yippee-ay-yayed. Pleased as punch, Old Thunder stretched out and galloped down the middle. *Clippity, clippity, clippity!* What in tarnation? We zoomed around Winnie Oates and Lightning, and then . . .

Old Thunder took the lead! His hooves, light as wind-sifted flour, never even touched the ground as he sailed over the finish line.

The announcer held aloft a blue ribbon and called out, "And now, the winner—

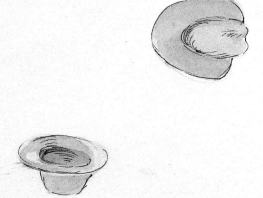

Miss Raney Cloud's whirlwind of a horse, Old Thunder!"

Old Thunder and Raney Cloud

But what beat all was this: What do you think those Washita County Fair judges did?

Why, they gave me a blue ribbon for best horse feed . . . for my Sooner High-Energy Horse Biscuits!

Well, I do declare, I was mighty proud. Mighty proud, indeedy!